MORTALITY BIRDS

MORTALITY BIRDS

~A Dovecote of Fictions~

TIMOTHY DODD
&
STEVE LAMBERT

Introduction by Sheldon Lee Compton

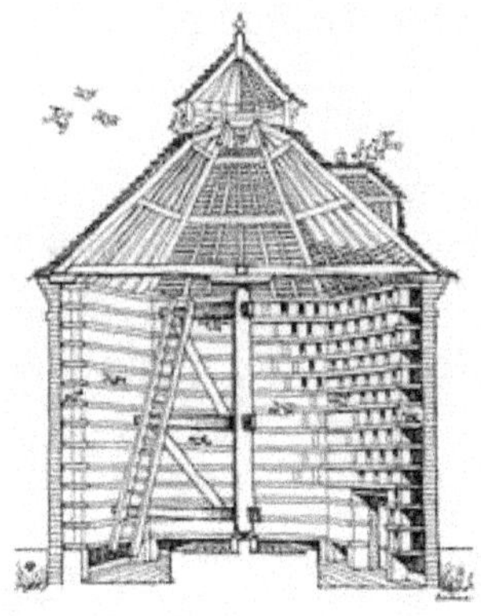

STHRNMST BKS | 2022 | Florida

For more information:
SouthernmostJournal@gmail.com

Published by Southernmost Books
Saint Augustine, FL

First Edition
ISBN: 978-0-578-28989-2

The following stories have appeared elsewhere: "A Minor Character" appeared in *New World Writing*; "Television Light" appeared in the story collection *Men in Midnight Bloom* (Cowboy Jamboree Press).

Cover and interior design: Gavin Stephen Lambert III

"Have you ever seen the skull of a snow bunting?"

—Halldor Laxness, *Under the Glacier*

Other Titles by Timothy Dodd

FICTION

Fissures and Other Stories
Men in Midnight Bloom

POETRY

Modern Ancient

Other Titles by Steve Lambert

FICTION

The Patron Saint of Birds
Philisteens

POETRY

Heat Seekers
In Eynsham (chapbook)
The Shamble

Contents

Introduction
"The trauma of being reminded..."

Sheldon Lee Compton

I first started buying Stephen King books in 1986, saving one dollar a day Monday through Friday to get the $5 needed for a book by Saturday. Signet paperbacks were $4.95 at that time and sold at a place a half hour from my house called The Book Nook. That was an enchanted time for me. And then came the day I bought *The Talisman*.

The Talisman was the first novel co-written by Stephen King and Peter Straub, another major and bestselling horror writer. I bought the book because King's name was on it. I had no idea who Straub was yet and, honestly, felt he was butting in where he wasn't needed. But I was ten and never read *The Talisman* and King and Straub knew then what was reinforced for me after recently reading Timothy Dodd and Steve Lambert's *Mortality Birds*: there are certain brains that work together in ways neither can separately.

I don't mean to say Steve and Tim can't write hell off the hinges on their own. They certainly can. What I mean to say is that when the two of them gradually leaned into this collaboration a new voice came through and the four stories here became

Mortality Birds, the golden hybrid of both writers and a project that truly began in an online creative writing course through the University of Texas at El Paso.

After their time together in the program at UTEP, the two kept in touch, leading to an invitation from Tim to do some traveling together this past year. After a pact of sorts to not talk writing during the trip, Tim went to Savannah and met up with Steve and after a look around they went to Steve's home in St. Augustine. As agreed, there wasn't too much talk of writing (with the brief exception of some chatting at Conrad Aiken's grave in Savannah) and both went back to their own day to day routines.

This trip together was in July, and it was as soon as September that Steve presented the idea of a collaboration. Like many cool things, it happened sort of by accident. It started with a discussion of how it would be interesting to write companion stories; not retellings but....Well, they couldn't think what to call them, but the idea was this: each writes a story that is a response to—or echo of—a story of the other's. Steve brought in Charles Baxter's concept of rhyming action and, together, they moved forward thinking of these stories as couplets. They would write stories that *rhymed.*

Baxter puts words to theory better than just about anybody and it's likely a happy coincidence that his theory for the narrative-echo, as he called it, would be found in writers such as Conrad Aiken, the same such author whose grave Tim and Steve visited together.

"A boy goes to a city park in the spring to fly a kite. The scene is infused with a kind of lyric innocence and bravery. The kite is yellow," Baxter wrote. "Conrad Aiken's stories are usually structured in this manner. Years later, when the boy has grown to be a man, he happens to walk into the same park and sees a young woman who is flying a kite. She's with another man, but her blouse is the same yellow."

One variation in this approach, the repetition, the narrative echo, is the book you're about to read. These stories are in rare dialogue and are nothing near what you may have read before. As Tim put it, they didn't want these stories to be "merely a constructed and contrived exercise."

Mortality Birds is anything but contrived. There's no shave and a haircut two bits within these pages, and there's galactically more going on than the basic sharing of a narrative. You'll feel it inside every sentence, moving about within the darker moments, the moments that almost hurt the heart to read. It is mortality these two writers are giving us here, the inescapable logic of it, the reality of it, the lonely and desperate moments when it seems mortality might chisel away our thick skins and send us ribboned away in gale winds beyond even the gods' control.

From the opening two stories, the call and response approach becomes evident and readers will see just how in tune these two writers are. In Steve's "A Minor Character" we are introduced to the character James Healy. Healy and his wife spend time with another couple and the relaxing evening disintegrates beneath the weight of Healy's drunken and damaged self-esteem. Steve closes the story with a chilling bedroom scene that is later teased out in Tim's following story "Fishmonger."

Here Tim starts where "A Minor Character" leaves off, with James in bed with his wife Rachel. Right away, as both he and Rachel come awake for the day, we're shown James's bleak state of mind, thinking to himself, "It seems there is nothing I want; only a lot I don't want. If we were right—if I was right—I'd float right into the bleak night." We move past that chilling scene and into one of what would typically be marital harmony, bacon and grits for breakfast. But the reader knows better, and it makes sense when we have James "trudging" down to breakfast. The day doesn't get much better for James and again, just as Steve did, Tim ends the story in a chilling way and a fantastic final two lines: "Truly, the flesh on my face remains soft. I, fishmonger."

These stories are connected both in the larger view of theme—dying and feeling cast out from normal society—but also in details woven throughout. There is a tapestry that slowly and satisfyingly forms to offer readers a well-earned sense of completion.

Mortality is not only the idea of death or the knowledge of death but also the trauma of being reminded of it. This book has the potential to offer reminders for years to come for readers of every age. Very much as critics say of *The Catcher in the Rye*, the *Mortality Birds* you might read this year will likely not be the *Mortality Birds* you'd read ten or twenty years from now. This says complete sets about what these men have accomplished.

Grateful to know both talented writers well, I had the chance to interview Tim for *Plumb*. It was during the interview he addressed his early process, one he would carry with him into collaborating with Steve. He spoke in most detail of his teen years when he first considered writing.

"I didn't feel right to say anything, and thought it more important to observe, listen, read, and move about (travel) as much as possible," Tim said. "More than anything else that decision developed my voice, both as a person and eventual writer, in a natural and authentic way. And with that as well, I should say it's important to me that the stories come from somewhere beyond my own self and ego."

Tim had stated an approach with those words many years out from the eventual completion of *Mortality Birds*, but it might well have been a mission statement for the book itself. There's a quiet confidence inside these pages shared between two writers who care deeply about working together to offer us an entirely unique work. As James Healy concludes in the opening story, "It's nothing. It's just predictable. So fucking predictable." Timothy Dodd and Steve Lambert are in no way predictable, and you can sense they worked incredibly hard to make sure they weren't.

They succeeded.

The book you're about to read will be a unique experience. What is predictable will still surprise, what is tragic will be shown with such beauty that tragedy will become poetry, what is left unsaid will be shown through the purest imagery and in the purest fashion.

Beyond self and ego.

Sheldon Lee Compton
January 1, 2022
Pikeville, Kentucky

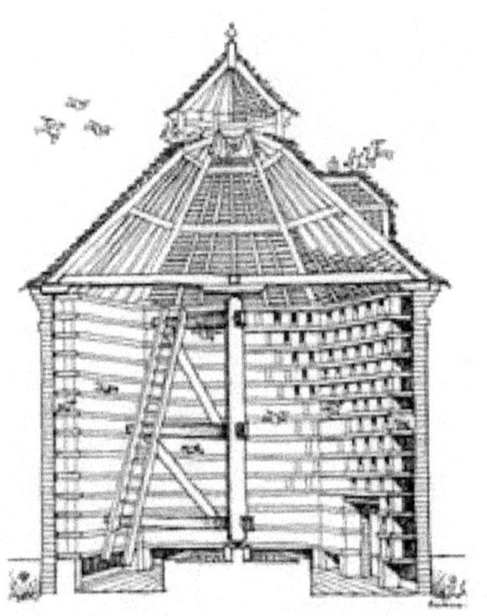

AA

A Minor Character

"You gotta love the Sharon Lipschutzes of the world," says James. "You really do."

Rachel turns the page of her book and looks over at her husband. "Sharon Lipschutz?" She squints at the cover of his book, even though she already knows what book it is. "She the tennis girl in the Eskimo one?"

"No, she's the little girl in 'Bananafish' who sits on the piano when Seymour plays. Makes Sybil Carpenter jealous."

"Sybil Carpenter? The little girl on the beach? What does she have to be jealous of? She's more of a main character."

"Yeah," he says. "God, her mother's terrible. There are three mothers in the story and they're all pretty terrible in some way. Gotta think that's intentional."

Rachel sighs and turns back to her book, a popular romance novel. She likes those best and is unapologetic about it. "I don't want to do any thinking with my reading," she always says when James criticizes her.

James goes back to reading, too, but only his favorite part, the end.

Rachel closes the book on her finger again and turns back to her husband.

"That reminds me. Don't forget about tomorrow."

"Tomorrow? Will there even be a tomorrow?"

He puts the book in his lap.

"Tomorrow's Memorial Day. The beach. We're meeting the Davises after lunch. I know how you like to forget these things."

"Shit, the beach."

He flops open the book. He reads the last paragraph, over and over. It's perfect, he thinks. No wasted words.

Rachel watches her husband read. She likes to watch him do simple, seemingly sane things like this. Life, she thinks, is full of deferments and strategies. Coping mechanisms.

"How many times have you read that stupid story now, I wonder."

"It's something like my ninetieth time. If you'd let me finish."

He adjusts the book in his hand and clears his throat.

"Seriously. How many?"

"In reality?" He closes the book and looks at the cover. He puts the palm of his hand on the book as if he were swearing on it. "Maybe twenty times, all the way through. Sometimes I just read bits."

James Healy doesn't hate the beach. But he doesn't like being there. When he is at the beach, he feels like a wrongly placed puzzle piece, or an oddly cast extra in a movie. He brought this up to Rachel once and she assured him that the only thing making him stand out was his behavior. "If you'd stop acting weird, no one would even notice you." But if he could go there and be unseen, he'd feel very drawn to it: the foamy waves breaking hard against the flat grit of the beach and gently receding; the seagulls cawing and the kids screaming; and the scents too: the fishy-salty smell of the ocean, the seemingly ever-present coconut smell of sunblock; the way it's always windy at the beach, and the tiny grey fishing and shrimping boats that slide along the taut string of the horizon. And who could object to the bathing beauties? They alone are reason to be fond of the place. Where else might you find young people lying and walking around as if there's nothing ugly in the world? All these things he likes, even loves, and would experience, again and again, if only he could be there and be invisible.

But the one good thing, the one saving grace of this particular trip to the beach, is that it will be Memorial Day, which means the beach will be crowded with awkward, overweight, ogling, farmer-tanned, middle-aged townies just like himself. He figures he can blend in at least.

The Healys arrive first. They always arrive first to everything because Rachel has a phobia of being late. This, at times, seems to James like an obscure form of masochism, as she is married to a man who doesn't seem to care if they ever arrive anywhere at all. After they get everything set up, James and Rachel sit in their chairs under a large hot-pink umbrella.

Rachel opens up a fashion magazine and James holds onto his book and looks around.

"Couldn't we have gone to the movies or something? Our first outing with these people and you pick the beach?"

"We *could* have gone to the movies. But we didn't. And I didn't pick the beach. They picked the beach. Believe me, I wouldn't have picked the beach." She gives him a long, knowing look. "Anyway, it's a perfectly normal place for people to go to. Look around you." She slaps the magazine against her thigh. "Are you going to be like this the whole time?"

"All right, all right..." He opens his book but can't focus on it. Any time someone walks by he can't help looking at them. (As he's predicted, a large sampling of the suburban middle-aged crowd the beach.) A young, college-aged couple is camped out immediately to their right. The young man sits in a reclining chair reading a men's fitness magazine and his girl lies on her stomach with her bathing-suit top undone, her arms crossed under her head, her eyes closed. James can see the delicate pearly part of the side of her breast. Looking at it gives him a jittery, speedy feeling. He tries not to look, but he can't help glancing over periodically. The guy catches him and stares James down.

The Davises show up about half an hour later. The Davises are, quite conceivably, the last available couple in the Healy's social pool, and James knows it. Rachel has made sure he understands that, and he doesn't want to let Rachel down.

They're a good-looking, energetic couple, around the same age as the Healys. Matt Davis is tall and brawny and intelligent with, it quickly becomes clear, a strong appreciation of the naughty and off-color. James doesn't yet know if he has been one or not, but there is something of the frat boy about Matt. Grace is petite but sturdy and has a great sense of humor, but James suspects she might be a bit of a hypochondriac. Whenever someone brings up an ailment or injury, Grace, it seems, has suffered from the very same thing (but only worse, of course) at some point in her apparently perilous life. Both the Davises played a sport in college and don't show the slightest signs of having let themselves go in early middle age. And Grace carries around with her a bag of assorted creams and lotions she rubs on herself from time to time, very casually, like someone scratching an itch, or taking a sip of a drink. Consequently, she's always very moist looking. They are, in fact, a new kind of couple for the Healys. Until now they'd hung around people more or less like themselves, the dilettante crowd; vaguely artsy people with some variety of stalled creative aspiration.

In contrast to the athletic and energetic Davises, James thinks, he and Rachel look rather plain—sort of bland and muted. James has a boyish charm, even if it is beginning to fade a little in his late-thirties, and Rachel has a certain cute-nerd quality that can be very alluring and even erotic, but, to James, next to the Davises, they are both somewhat boring to look at.

Grace sits to the left of Rachel and Matt sits to the right of James. Matt looks around before pulling a can of beer from his cooler and pouring it into a Solo cup. He hands James the cup of beer and says, "Pass it down." Once they all have a cup of beer in hand or at foot, they sit quietly for a good while, listening and watching and drinking. Collectively, they are the very picture of relaxation. James remembers the semi-topless girl and steals a glance. She's in almost the same position, and her man is too.

"When you get a chance, take a look to your right. Don't let the ape see you do it though."

Matt puts on his sunglasses and then glances to his right.

"Sweet Jesus," he whispers.

James goes for another look and gets caught in the act again.

"Goddamnit! That's twice now."

"You filthy bastard!" Matt giggles and gives James a soft punch on the shoulder. "Totally inappropriate....You should be ashamed."

"What are you two fussing about over there?" says Grace. She hands her empty cup across and James takes it and hands it to Matt. Matt does a scan up and down the beach and refills it.

They enjoy themselves at the beach so much that before leaving they make plans to meet up— after going home and cleaning up and having dinner—for drinks at the Healy's. James is even kind of into the idea. Everyone is in high spirits and looking forward to furthering the good times later in the evening.

Rachel makes sure James wears something decent. Left to make his own choices, he might pick something that doesn't match, or a shirt with a hole in it. He has many shirts with holes in them, and delights in wearing them, almost as if the holes were badges or medals. He sometimes even points out the holes to company, which embarrasses Rachel. "I've had this shirt so long it's giving out on me." He'll have a big smile on his face. Even many of his "dress shirts" are threadbare. The problem is that he hates going clothes shopping. And there are so many reasons he hates going clothes shopping that there is no one quick remedy. Consequently, Rachel ends up buying most of his clothes, and he ends up hating most of what she buys. When he finds himself liking a shirt or pair of pants he wears them religiously and develops an almost emotional attachment and it becomes very difficult for him to part with them.

The Davises bring some expensive tequila and suggest doing shots.

"Just one for me," says James. He doesn't mind the stuff, but he doesn't feel comfortable being too drunk. Rachel nods emphatically. "Oh, just one for me, too," she adds. She holds up the shot glass. She smiles and tosses it back.

Being that these are two couples who hardly know each other, their conversation quickly progresses from the incidental to the more personal. The booze helps. This is something that James and Rachel have to be cautious about. Sober it's easy to control a situation and keep things focused on surface matters. But buzzed or drunk, too much could easily get said. The *whys* and *hows* of things can come spilling out, not even purposely, and a first pleasant night with new friends can easily turn into a one-time thing.

"We've definitely moved around a lot," says Matt. "But that's the nature of the field. Jobs are usually contract only and don't often last longer than a few years." He looks sympathetically at his wife. She touches his hand and grimaces, as if to say, yes, it is tough, but I understand.

"I've never lived anywhere else," says James. "I was born here and, except for a little travelling in my early twenties, that's it. Isn't that pathetic?" He looks at Rachel and her face is wrung up, but with a tense smile. It's an "oh, my silly husband" look, which is familiar to James. It functions almost as a visual cue for him. Too many of these and he probably needs to be more careful about what he says, needs to dial things back a bit.

"I think it's great," says Grace. "I've never had that—not even as a child. I was an Air Force brat. Every four years...off we went."

"At least you got to travel—see some great places. I bet you lived overseas." Rachel's face lights up.

"We lived in Italy for four years, when I was in elementary school. I was very young, so I didn't really appreciate it."

Rachel points her beer at her husband. "James has a penchant for self-deprecation. He's being modest. He's been all over the world. Went off to Alaska when we were dating. Lived there for three months. He's been to Japan, Taiwan, China...all over."

"Wow! Alaska." Says Grace. "That must have been an adventure. I've always wanted to go."

"It was...okay, I guess. I was there during the summer."

"See what I mean? If he was drunk, he'd talk your ear off about it."

"Well, then," says Matt. He holds up the tequila bottle and smiles. "Let's get to work."

"Oh, no," say Rachel and James, almost in unison.

"Come on." Matt sets up four shot glasses and starts pouring. He is not going to take no for an answer. Rachel curses herself for saying something so irresponsible. James begins to think his suspicions about Matt have been correct: this man is a grown-up frat boy. Matt the Frat Boy, he says to himself.

By around ten they've worked their way onto the back porch. James wanted to smoke, which is something he does only when he is drinking. He buys a pack occasionally and it usually lasts him months. When James says, "I don't know about anyone else, but I could use a smoke," Grace says, "Oh, I want one! I want one!" Rachel and Matt look at each other and make disapproving faces. Rachel knows that James' wanting to smoke is a red flag.

It's very humid out, but not hot. Halfway into his cigarette, James is feeling relaxed and fairly drunk. He notices Rachel staring at him and he winks at her. She raises her eyebrows and looks away. He gets the message but is drunk enough now not to care.

"You must work out or something." James leans into his Adirondack chair and takes a drag of his smoke. "You're a pretty big guy."

"Yeah, well. I go to the gym every morning." It's obvious from his tone of voice he doesn't want to make a big deal out of it.

"Yeah, me too." James leans over and puts the cigarette butt out in the ashtray on a table between he and Grace.

"Yes, I can tell." Matt leans back into his chair and shows everyone an amiable, boozy smile.

"Can you? Can you *really* tell?" James' tone is harsh. He stands up and pulls back his shirt sleeve and flexes his arm.

Rachel's the first to laugh. Grace and Matt quickly join in.

James puts his arm back down and starts laughing too.

"You've never seen anything like that, have you, Grace?" James picks up his beer and takes a swig of it.

"Oh, dear God, no! It was frightening!" Everyone lets out loud, loose laughs.

"I'm a lucky lady," says Rachel and puts her head in her hand. She erupts, again, in laughter and sighs. "He's all mine, Grace, so back off!"

"Man, those really are some guns you got there, Jimmy," says Matt.

James stops laughing abruptly and so does Rachel.

"Well that's just disappointing," says James.

"What? Did I say something?" Matt's hands grab onto the armrests of his chair.

Rachel looks nervously over at her husband and sees his posture slacken.

"Nothing," says James. "It's nothing. It's just predictable. So fucking predictable. Big muscly guy makes fun of the skinny guy. What's next a wedgie? A swirlie? You gonna try fucking my wife?"

Grace puts her cigarette out. She has a rigid smile on her face, as if her lips have gotten stuck that way. Matt looks over at Rachel and silently mouths *what?*

They all go back inside, except for James. He sits on the porch until the Davises leave. He only comes in once it starts raining, and he goes straight to the bedroom.

Rachel is asleep with the light on, bunched up under the covers, only her head exposed. He doesn't understand how he can be so hot when she is so cold. James walks into the closet and lifts up a pile of folded pants from a high shelf. He feels around until his hand knocks into it. In the beginning, Rachel didn't like having it in the house but James convinced her that it would be a good idea and that eventually she would not only get used to it but it would also come to make her feel safe. And he'd been right. She told him as much once. He gets into bed next to his sleeping wife and reclines against the headboard. How can she be under all those covers when he's sweating in nothing but a t-shirt and boxers? He reaches over and opens the top drawer of his bedside table. He takes a single bullet out of the drawer and puts it into one of the cylinder chambers. He sticks the barrel into his mouth and angles the tip of it against the top of the back of his throat, just the way he's always imagined he would. Rachel stirs. He quickly puts the gun under the covers. She lifts her head and squints her eyes toward James. "What are you doing?" she rasps. "Just getting into bed," he says. "Go back to sleep." She puts her hand out in his direction and searches for him with it. He touches her hand. It's very cold. When she falls asleep he gets up, puts the gun away, and gets back into bed, pulls her close. Rachel coos and presses her cold body into James' warm body. "Good night," says James, and Rachel mumbles something that sounds like *everything's okay.*

—Steve Lambert

Fishmonger

Rachel is the silhouette next to me, in soft nightgown, and I'm ashamed to admit that sometimes I imagine her waking up aged and frail, in a different body altogether. Or never waking up at all. Where would it put me? She is my only tangible and has harbored for so long, with much strength, given me a strange and sad kind of semi-sanctuary. One that's had its moments of happiness as well, I must admit, but maybe even that is a ceiling keeping me from drowning this long rust.

I lie stiff in the shallow of our bed, eyes walking the shadowy perimeter of our bedroom window. It seems there is nothing I want; only a lot I don't want. If we were right—if I was right—I'd float right into the bleak night. In the vestige of my gaze are the outlines of nightstand books: precarious stacks of paper and words; ideas and creations from heads made of ore, currency, straw, and bone; eyes that watch when I put the gun away; lungs that exhale and voices that laugh or say I haven't even been to war; minds that hatch poems about destiny in their wily, written, reconciled kind of way, carving broken sentences on my cave walls.

I bleed all my ideas until Rachel wakes up several minutes before her alarm goes off, the room itself sitting up in muted morning light. She's not even groggy. Lifts and stretches, rejuvenated. Energized. Sharing some sort of perfect synergy with sleep. Ready to go. As if it's the day we're setting off for France. Or Long Island. As if it's the morning of our own wedding. Or the day that she'll win the lottery. And knows it. I close my eyes to feign a minor sleep.

An hour later the smell of bacon and eggs gets to me. Rachel doesn't have to call. I trudge out of the bedroom in my t-shirt and boxers, scratch the back of my neck and push my hair over to the side. In my yawn I pretend to believe in the contentedness of
middle class dependencies.

"Morning," Rachel says. "Good morning, my fish out of water."

I slide down the hallway to the bathroom, leaving the door open as I piss and rinse off the night scum from my face. That's the best of Rachel right there, I think, whether she's aware of it or not. My coach. Sweeping nothing under the rug, but telling me in her own sweet way that it doesn't really matter much—life goes on. She tells me what I can't even believe myself, tries her beautiful best to push out those brooding fragments and shards stuck in my skull.

"Sleep well?" I ask her in the kitchen, pouring my coffee. Instead of an answer, I hear the blender working on her morning smoothie. I sit down and dish out the fruits of mechanized farming onto my plate: a clump of scrambled eggs, another clump of cheesy grits, and four strips of bacon. I get in a couple bites of each—

> —the trash has to be taken out
> —we're out of onions...and eight other things put on a list
> —the Billinghams complained of our tree leaning onto their property
> —she has a dental appointment and it's been so long that I should go, too
> —could I drop off a bag of plums for her mother
> —booked us a hotel in Houston for late February
> —I am not to talk about Squidbillies anymore
> —the Gators will be at Kentucky tomorrow and people are coming over to watch the game
> —I need to grill the burgers and hot dogs since I'm the only one who doesn't care if the quarterback gets sacked eight times and throws four interceptions

"You should move to Canada," Eric Beetle often tells me. He's an old migrant from Poughkeepsie who lives three houses down from us. "They hardly have football. And maybe not even sports. At least not that much."

For years I've tried to learn how to sort of swallow it all and skirt the line—like knowing how to say something, anything, when your boss is talking to you. It's always a mixture of personal nonsense and all things job related, isn't it? Always.

"Why can't you just ask me about 'Bananafish' again?" I finally say.

"Bananafish?"

"Yeah. You know, the book you could carry to a Florida football game. Bright orange and blue cover."

"The one you were reading again last night? *Ninety Stories* or whatever?"

"Yes, that one. *Nine Stories.* 'A Perfect Day for Bananafish' is the first story in the collection."

"But it's still in the bedroom, hon." I pause my chewing, shake my head. "Anyway, what's a bananafish? I've wondered about it before but didn't want to ask while you're reading. We don't have them here, do we?"

"Sure we do. They're everywhere. Especially Florida. Even more in Orlando."

"Really? Have you eaten them? Can you eat them? How are they?"

"Not the best. Kind of blubbery. They eat far more than they're eaten."

Rachel doesn't have the time to question me. She puts her plates in the sink and is off to the bedroom. I dab at the rest of my food while she glides about, loading up the hatchback: two briefcases, two laptops, a book bag, a package of thirty-two plastic bottles of water, a lunch kit, sneakers, a box of something else I can't identify. Probably more technology. After more reminders and an "I love you," she pulls the door to the garage closed and I'm left standing in that odd silence that's as stuffy, sticky, as a Florida summer.

I put my fork down. I don't know what to do. I don't want to do anything—sleep, eat, shower, Salinger, TV, music. I've never wanted to want like some of these other people, like bananafish, but it would be nice to want something.

The telephone rings. I know it's my mother-in-law, and I know she wants to talk to *me*, not anyone else. Otherwise, she'd call Rachel on her cell. Mrs. Sumter's the only one who calls our landline, something we still have "just in case," Rachel says. Her mother lives in Fort Myers. I've been there once and don't remember anything about it.

And I don't pick up the phone because James Healy says horrible things to horrible people. James Healy dumps new plates in the trash, reads tombstones like they're comics, and reminds people, all too often, that they're going to die.

I walk to the bedroom and take the gun from the closet again, remove my wedding ring and place it under the folded pants: Rachel will not be any part of this. I will not bring a chair. I will not bring a beach towel or umbrella, hot pink or otherwise. I will not bring sunscreen, rafts, bestseller paperbacks or fashion magazines. There will be no flip-flops. I will be neither late, nor early, but I will go to the edge, to the water, without their communion, free of the human cacophony. I will not see bikini crafts plastic floats crucifix sag and flab. I will not see the gouging of shells and crustacean. I will feel the nourishment of the sun, blood of the ocean, and the breath of life teeming there.

Driving east, I stop off Route 20 for a brewery just before Palatka—some new place...Swampfest   or something. I park and walk into a spacious bar riding the now common aesthetic of warehouse meets comfortable rustic, all laid out in pine so freshly cut I can smell the wood. A few customers sit outside on the deck with their drinks. Inside, it's just me and the bartender, a young twenty-something who tells me he's new at this himself. I order the Alligator Bite IPA and position myself at the bar to limit peripheral vision.

"I like your shirt," he says, setting the glass in front of me. I don't reply, putting a nose to the thick, white, citrusy head and taking a drink before looking down to remember I'm wearing an old Dreadstar tee with a hole just under my left armpit. I drink fast, ready to order a second when the bartender's phone rings. He pulls it from his belt clip and looks down, turns his back to me and takes the call.

"Who was it?" I ask after his short conversation is finished.

"My mother," he answers with a laugh. "She lives in Cassadaga and, well, you know how they are. She's got a seventh sense to match the sixth one."

I smile, give the kid some credit. "You wanting a witty comeback?"

He snickers. "Nah. Want another beer?"

"Yeah. Same thing."

"She asked me if I had a customer now," he says a minute later, plopping down my second glass before leaning onto the bar. "She was carrying this nudge or something in her voice. All kinds of implications. Like she's got some kind of special insight. That's exactly why I had to move out. She's a wack job."

"Yeah, well, mothers...you know." I readjust on the stool, feel the muzzle of the pistol rubbing against my hip. "What's your name by the way?"

"Matt."

"And what kind of insight did Matt's mom give to her son?"

"She said she'd received a warning. Premonition I think she calls it."

"Okay."

"Said I'll have a middle-aged, male customer today that's up to no good. Someone who maybe likes to trespass and can be violent. What a nut. Then she adds, 'but he's not a hunter.'"

I take a good gulp of my beer, figure I'll be on my way when it's done. "Maybe she's got me on her mind. I might be the violent, trespassing type."

"And you don't hunt?"

"I'd hunt if there was a human season. With bare hands. I'd snap goddamn heads off."

Matt gives a little grunt-laugh, more awkward than irked or offended. His phone rings again. He looks at it, but doesn't answer. "Yep. Her again."

"Sounds like she's got some Sophie Portnoy in her."

"Who?"

"This crazy character in a Philip Roth book."

"Don't know her. Or him."

"Do you read? Anything?"

"Mostly movies."

"That's not reading."

"I know," Matt says, turning his head toward customers who've just entered, approaching the counter. I turn, too, see two, jeans-clad women younger than Matt.

"Those your sisters?" I ask him.

He laughs and slides down the bar two spots from me, greeting the women aggressively. Some would call it friendly. They order something and Matt tosses them a "You got it."

"I guess I should have asked you what's good since it's our first time here," the girl seated closest to me says.

"It's everyone's first time here," I reply.

"Why? I'm Tara, by the way."

"Why? You haven't seen the 'Grand Opening' signs plastered over every wall and orifice?"

I mostly ignore the long reply about her and a best friend being off from work and driving down to Vero Beach. Matt sets their drinks down, then retreats to the other side of the bar, resumes his texting.

"What's your job, by the way?"

"Fishmonger," I answer.

"Like a fisherman?"

"No. Not a fisherman. Not a Polonius. I'm a goddamn fishmonger. I sell fish."

"Oh, you're a salesman."

"Yes, I'm a fishmonger. I peddle carcass. Millions of creatures pulled from the ocean where their own gills will do them no more damn good. I take them out of their own living habitat for dollars. I help put them on your plate so Melody can ask if you want cocktail or tartar sauce."

"Sounds interesting."

"You think so? Well, yeah, I've done it all over Florida and coastal Georgia. Salmon in Alaska. Walleye and muskie in West Virginia. Deep sea fishing off Orchid Island in Taiwan for recreation. Lots and lots of fish guts on my hands."

"I've been to Virginia Beach."

"I said West Virginia."

"Oh, okay."

"One time I pulled a fish with red eyes out of Summersville Lake in West Virginia. Red and metallic like tail lights. Something in the water there from all the chemical plants. When I got to opening the fish's mouth, it had a big, rubbery human tongue. Flopped around like the ticker of a busted odometer. I'm sure we're going to be seeing more of that here, too, soon enough. Here in Florida."

Rachel calls them big fibs. And me a big liar. But if truth is what mattered, none of us would still be sitting here. What most people want is a good story, a good tingle, whether it hurts or not. I'm no different. And we all engage in the telling in one form or other. Smoothing over the dirt so we can't see the casket or its truths lying deep down in the earth. Sometimes I'm a piano player. Once I was an Olympic figure skater who couldn't win a medal. I've been a Baton Rouge firefighter and a hairdresser in Lansing. Next day I was a mercenary overthrowing the government in Managua.

I drain the last quarter of my beer as Matt hurries over, pushing through the echoes of Tara's reply. Maybe I've given her a lot to run with. I toss a twenty onto the bar. "Keep the change, Matt. All the best."

I turn north onto A1A, crawl my vehicle onto the ferry crossing St. John's River and head for Big Talbot Island, Boneyard Beach. Rachel and I went there once several years ago, but she didn't like it. It's a graveyard of live oak and cedar, sun-bleached corpses spread across the sand rising in twisted, reaching limbs.

I swipe my card at the self-serve pay station and park, get out of the car. I find the dirt trail at the edge of the lot leading to a spot where there's a cut in the twenty-foot cliff overlooking the beach. The sun is stronger now nearing noon, beating down on a man with no cloud cover, and I descend to the beige sand, to a shore free of wishful, sanitized bodies. The little piping plovers skitter at the edge of the water with shrills of warning. A great blue heron—its ancientness—stands a bit further out, ready to spear. I fit myself into a comfortable seat wedged between two waist-high pieces of driftwood. Blue crabs scurry around in their tidal pools. I look out past Nassau Sound to the Atlantic Ocean, its water long and the sky carrying infinity. A capsized cargo ship, the MV Global Pearl, is a blurred and wrecked titan lying not too far in the distance, right off the tip of Amelia Island. It overturned nearly two years ago, just after leaving port with over three thousand automobiles stacked on its decks. A salvage crew is still demolishing it, removing sections of the ship piece by piece. It is one mammoth bananafish.

I think how Tommy Capri, Rachel's manager at work, would shit his pants if he saw this barge. Tommy has everything in the right place—his suit, his tie, his garage door, his mug, his little words and his nasal mucus. There's nothing quite so distasteful. Maybe not even this monstrosity of metal soaking out in the water. But Rachel likes him. She appreciates his predictability and believes he's something akin to security. "He gets the job done," she says. "Far more than most." Tommy would be coming over to the house for the game tomorrow. He hates Kentucky for some reason—the whole state, I believe. He has his own stories.

On the sand, at the ocean, between driftwood and a capsized ship, I think about sick things like Tommy Capri. I feel no relief in knowing every single Tommy Capri will decay the same as me, right down to our gums and pelvis. I take out the gun and stand up, move down to the water and feel the briny liquid start to seep into my shoes, then soak my legs as I walk further out, each slow step increasingly weighted.

I stop and look down into the waist-deep water, majestically clear no matter what the MV Global

Pearl has drained into it. The whiting dart about, flitting around in the blue that might flow all the way to Namibia. Or Ireland. Or India. I don't know where the ocean currents go. I am only a trader of dead fish. You wouldn't believe these silver schools could ever make it to places so distant, and maybe they don't, but you wouldn't believe the swallow-tailed kites get down to Machu Picchu either. Our sense of geography is not the same as the animals'. I think they very much know what they know. Which on most days is far more than I'm capable of.

I cock the gun, lift and place its muzzle on my temple. I don't believe this gun will much follow the currents, the animals and their migration patterns, or me. It will sink. In copper, tin, and zinc. In weighted bullet. *In water.*

I tell myself another story: a story of lowering the pistol, then whipping it behind my head. And with a great sling, I lose my balance and fall into this ocean, the gun flying toward the capsized boat, although it of course never makes it there. Instead, it comes down gleaming in the sun, heavy, with a relatively minor splash, entering the water of a magnificent ocean that stretches to other continents. The fish momentarily scatter and recede, then return. The gun, too, jumps—up out of the water growing fins, and joins the fish, swims away.

In the distance, on the beach, perhaps walking toward me, I see someone who might hear my story, whether they are listening or not. I am unsure of their age, and gender is undefined; purpose—who could know? But they are on the sand, upright and alone, moving near the cadavers of trees that have made their rest, limbs like the skeletons of fish, made up of hundreds of tiny bones, hard and brittle.

It is too late for me. I drop. I go down. In my small time, little place. In search of.

The fish momentarily scatter and recede. Then return. Let them feed. It is their chance and they have earned what I have not.

Truly, the flesh on my face remains soft. I, fishmonger.

—Timothy Dodd

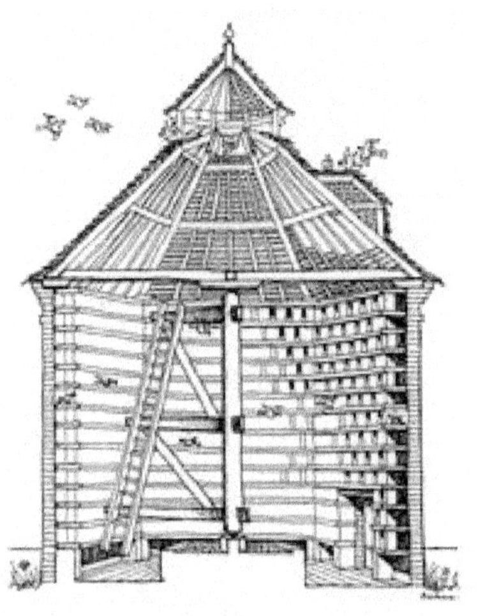

BB

Television Light

It's one of those nights when it's hard to even see your own foot stepping in front of you. No cars on the road. No headlights. Too late for fireflies. There's no porch light on, and a feeble crescent moon is stuck behind the mountains. You'd have to be nocturnal to make something of the moment.

But that's outside, and I'm going inside. Entering through the basement window hidden by beetled weeds and half-emptied cans of paint stacked against the wall. Pushing into the void of the utility room. I land on the dryer and roll to the floor, get to my feet and navigate through the blackness and years of accumulated clutter. Up to the living room. Stairs creaking.

Turning on every light I can, I start to believe he isn't here at all. But then I find him. Lying on his back on the kitchen floor, tucked in the corner between refrigerator and pantry. Wearing his house clothes, hands down at his sides, his head almost turned backwards. Wounds and cuts sending a trail of dried blood down his cheek like a state with two panhandles. His eyes are closed, but he's breathing. I touch his shoulder, straighten his crooked neck, and say his name three times. The best eyes of anyone in our family open blue, but his face says his mind has drifted to other places.

"You fall?"

"Maybe."

"Let's get you to the sofa."

"Floor's fine." The voice is faint and shaky, but the words are clear, precise.

"Let me get you a pillow at least." I turn the corner to the living room, pick up a cushion and bed sheet folded on the sofa, take them back and get them under him.

"Cup of water," he says.

I stand up and flick on the spigot, put a cup under it until it's half full. I lift his neck just enough for his lips to meet the water as I tip the cup. He drinks a couple mouthfuls then lets his head back down.

"What else?"

"My pipe."

"You shouldn't stay on this floor, Pops."

"I'm fine. I'm dying. Just talk to me."

"Let me call an ambulance."

"Don't do that to me." He's breathing heavy and belaboring the words, but stubborn as usual, insistent to get them out. "Let things shoot...through the sky. While the hills are quiet."

I don't reply.

"Go easy...on the funeral, okay? No big sermon...hot air."

"Okay, Pops. I understand."

"How you get in here? I thought I locked...bust a window?"

"Yeah," I lie. "I'll replace it."

He doesn't seem to mind. "Talk to me."

"About what, Dad?"

"Anything. Tell me a...story. One I've...heard before."

I tell him about the time we drove down to Welch, ate biscuits and gravy at a little corner cafe. Tell him how we looked through the dusty window of an out-of-business dental office there, its antiquated X-ray machine and reclining exam chair still inside, and a hundred or more pink, dental casts dumped out on countertops, spilling onto the floor. He listens with his eyes closed and a little smile.

I tell him the story he'd told me himself, about going into Charleston with his father to buy cans of paint. How his daddy would stop off at a little store in Clendenin to place a phone call, have the proprietor dial for him because he didn't know how to do it himself.

And the telephone rings. Dad doesn't move or speak—maybe it's part of the story to him. I stand up from my crouch and go over to the phone that's hung from the wall since my childhood.

The recording pops on: "I know you're there so you better pick up for your own damn good."

Judy's never called my father's house since we separated. I think how I'm not accepting the precedent, but then pick up the phone anyway. "Yeah?"

"I figured you were over there," she says, slurring her words.

"Yeah. So? Visiting your own father a crime now?" I try to sound nonchalant, or feisty, but I know nothing good can come.

"Well, that hungry, hungry hippo of a girlfriend of yours said she thought you'd gone to see your dad. On account of his condition and all."

"Yeah, right."

"And I'm coming over."

"I don't have any cash on me now, Judy."

"Since when did you claim you did have it? But surely you've got cute little checks and credit cards, don't you Conrad? Sure you do. Or borrow from your damn father. Not my care how you get the money, but you missed another payment and I'm not sitting around drinking Sunkist all day waiting on your goddamn dead presidents."

I put my free hand up on the wall and lean over the telephone, lower my voice a bit. "Judy, look, it's not the time and place. Pops isn't doing well."

"Oh yeah? Well I don't care if he's dying. I ain't doing well either. Now listen. I'm only going to say this once. I'm coming over and I'm coming over now. I'm gonna knock nicely on the front door one time when I get there. One time. Regular volume. And you've got one whole minute to come and open up. Counting by Mississippis. If that door ain't open by then, I'll start banging. Louder and louder until you decide it's enough or I wake up your Pops and he comes let me in. Understand?"

"Judy, please. I'll pay you extra next..." The phone line clicks.

I walk back over to Pops running my hand through my hair. I kneel down beside him again—his breathing has stopped. I turn my head and put my ear to his mouth and nose. I curse. I curse Judy. What does it mean to be left with your father dead on the floor in the middle of the night when even the hour isn't known? I put my head on his chest and say his name, try to forget where I am.

When the promised knock on the front door comes, I stride out of the kitchen. I turn the lights off and pass the living room to the entrance, yank the door open.

"I hope you're satisfied," I say. I look into eyes that swirl like doped planets, like the smoke drifting up off her cigarette is coming from somewhere inside her head. "Dad is dead."

"I hope he told you to give me my money."

"You're a wreck. Enough scabs on you to play Tiddlywinks for hours."

She walks past me, breathes out more of her smoke and turns on some lights. "So you gonna drag me to safety, Con? Clean your own kitchen before pulling out someone else's pots and pans. Matter of fact, let me fix me a sandwich while you find my money. And I want all seven hundred twenty-two dollars and twelve cents of it, too."

I turn and follow her. "I told you I don't have it."

She stops. Glares at me like she's sizing up prey. Starts speaking in a low voice that's got the rhythm and intonation of a Southern Baptist minister quoting scripture at altar call. "You're gonna get that money for me right now, Con, or I'll walk out of here with your father's things. And I'll pawn every last bit of it until I have what is owed. Over seven hundred dollars' worth. The only thing I ain't gonna take with me is your thees and thous, Mr. Holy Pants."

She goes to the fridge, stumbles a little over Pops' body, but doesn't look down.

If Dad could stretch out his arm. Grab it, Pops. Grab her ankle and twist until it pops off her leg with the sound of a cork, leaving her foot in your hand.

The refrigerator door opens and the light from inside floods the room. "Dill pickles, okay. Cheese and baloney." She puts her weight on her left leg, staggers a bit. "Yellow mustard and an onion to slice just to give our dear old Conrad a little extra time to make his payment."

She pulls it all out of the fridge with a can of Coke and sets it on the kitchen counter, the door shutting behind her. A plate and a glass are pulled from the cabinet; a knife from a drawer. She brings it all to the table. Limping now. "Well what are you waiting for? I'm eating this sandwich and then you better have my money."

I turn and walk up the little set of stairs, go down the hall to Pops' bedroom, swing the door open. His old tube TV at the foot of his bed is on—volume turned down. Barn owls are on the screen, one glaring at me as I open the bottom drawer of his nightstand. I dig through the old papers and photographs, lift up three pocket New Testaments to get my hand on his checkbook. I sit back on the bed as the owl pushes a wood mouse further into its mouth. I date a pale yellow check and make it out to Judy, forge Dad's signature easily enough, and rip it out neatly along the perforation line.

"Here you go, parasite," I say, waving the check as I whisk back down the stairs. Judy's greedy eyes are on it, yanks it out of my hand when I get to the table, her sandwich mostly uneaten.

"I think this baloney might be old. Got a funny taste."

"Probably is. Dad hasn't been eating well the last couple of months. There's a whole bag of potatoes in the pantry that's turned green."

"He's nastier than you are. And I can't stand either of you."

"For Christ's sake, Judy. He's been sick."

She stands up from the table. "I don't care if he's got twenty-one different diseases as long as he wrote this check and saved his sorry son's ass. And don't be late next month either because I got a lawyer now."

"Shut up, Judy."

"Ain't you going to kick me out now?"

"Help me carry Pops up to his bed before you leave."

"What?"

I walk through the kitchen. "Over here. Come get his legs and I'll do the heavy lifting."

Judy putters as I position myself behind Pops' head, get my arms under his torso to make sure I can lift him. I reach farther down, down to his waist and curl a few fingers under his belt. My face is near his as I bend forward, hovering over him. Waiting on Judy, I see his wedding band is gone.

She lumbers over, stands beside him and grips one of his pant legs at the ankle like a lit up loser trying to lift a table by its tablecloth.

"You've got to help me a little more than that. Step over there below his feet and put your hands behind his heels, cup them and hold tight, then lift up like you'd pick up a log. I've got to get him up those stairs and down the hall."

"Why don't you just wake him up and tell him to go up there himself?"

"Judy, I...he's...Jesus, you got your check, now just help a minute."

She moves further down and picks Dad's legs up off the floor. I grunt and lift up his upper half, turn with my back to the stairs and start pulling him that way. I haven't gotten him even to the kitchen table when she lets go, leaving me to drag Pops across the floor like a rag doll.

"That can't feel good," Judy says.

I stop at the stairs, bend over further and lift again, pull him up the steps and then down the hallway. Judy follows like she's tracking an animal. I get Dad to the bedroom, prop him up against the bed, then one more heave to get him up to the mattress and drop in a jumble. I move his head onto the pillow and straighten his body, arrange his legs down the bed. Judy's standing next to me.

"He sick or something?"

"He's dead, dumbass. I already told you. If you'd stop popping pills for a day you might get a little perception beyond that of a moth."

"Shut up, Con. I just talked to him when you went upstairs. Said he didn't want a sandwich." I don't respond. An Eastern screech owl peers at us. "Does look pretty passed away now though."

We're standing together looking down at Dad. She's wobbly, and there's a bulge in her jeans' left pocket, the same place she stuffed the folded check I wrote her.

I pull up a small chair from the corner of the room and set it next to the bed. "Just a second, Judy. Sit here with him a minute while I go get a couple towels and another bed sheet."

"Well I'm not staying in a room alone with your father for very long, Con. You better be sure of that one. Hell, call an ambulance."

I walk out to clear my mind, go back downstairs thinking how to get Pops' damn wedding band out of Judy's pocket, wonder if she's taken anything else. She got the check, and that's all she'll get.

The hallway creaks under my stride as I return to the bedroom, pausing outside the door. Judy's talking to Pops. About a job at Fas-Chek.

"Con, he's making funny noises now," she says when she sees me. "Like forest noises. Birdie sounds."

"That's just the TV. Owls on the Discovery Channel or something," I say. "Judy, we need to switch that check I gave you with one Pops handed me a couple days ago. It's backdated. You're gonna have trouble cashing the one you got now since it's dated the same day he's died. Then you'll be fuming at me again. Give it back to me and I'll endorse this one here over to you," I say, taking a check out of my wallet that Dad had given me for paying his overdue gas bill. I figure as soon as she agrees, I'll doctor it up to look like eight hundred instead of three.

"Don't try and crook me, Con."

I hold the check out in front of me. More owls on the screen. A great horned swoops down from its winter perch to snag a chipmunk. "I'm not crooking anyone. If you run into trouble trying to cash today's check, I don't want to hear about it. Anyway, this one I've got here is a full eight hundred bucks."

"Well something's fishy. I don't trust you when you're trying to smell all bighearted."

"I don't give a damn about you," I say. "I'm just wondering if the bank is going to question how a dead man is writing checks. And if they do, you're not going to get your money and then you're going to blame me for it, like you always do."

"And this other one is for eight hundred?"

"Yeah."

"Let me see it."

"Jesus. It's right here," I say, waving it in front of her face. "You're not getting both of them. Give me the other one so I can tear it up, and then I'll sign this one over to you."

"Well you better understand I'm not leaving here without my money, Con, so let that sink in before you try to pull anything." She reaches three fingers into her front pocket—the jeans are tight. When she pulls the check out, Dad's ring shoots into the air, bounces on the floor and rolls under the bed. I stuff my check into my pocket and dive down on the ground, Judy right there with me, surprisingly agile. It's dark under the bed, of course, but I'm expecting the ring to glimmer. Instead, it's all dust bunnies and cobwebs as I bang heads with my genius ex-wife.

"You can't have my father's wedding ring and you know it," I say to her as I scour the ground, thinking it may have rolled under the bed and out the other side.

But then come the hoots and screeches. Like Pops has turned the TV up to its highest volume. Judy hits her head on the underside of the bed frame and I pull back, stand up to see a fluffy barred owl rise up, emerging from the wood of the bed's headboard, the ring shining in its beak as it flaps its wings and flies out of the bedroom down the hall.

Judy screams and starts cursing with words that don't make sense. Leaving her shaking on her knees, I stand up and scramble out of the room, figuring there's a chance the owl will drop the ring in the hallway. Otherwise, it could end up anywhere, never found—in the owl's stomach next to frog legs and mice bone, in the woods under a death cap. Even at Mom's graveside. I turn on the hall light and start scanning the ground.

"I wish you all would turn that television off," a voice calls out from the bedroom, vaguely sounding like Daddy's.

Judy runs out of the room past me, down the hallway—slowly to be honest, but as fast as she can muster. Her clenched fists sway back and forth under her chin like Rock 'em Sock 'em Robots. Footsteps trail down the stairs, through the living room, and out the front door.

I turn my head, look back down the hallway into Dad's bedroom. I see only the end of the bed, its sheets moving and fluttering like someone's trying to get comfortable under them. I smile—at the foot of the bed a little thin piece of pale yellow paper lies on the carpet. And then a forearm comes into view— and a hand, or claw, with long, sharp nails like talons—swooping down to pick up the check.

I call out Pops' name, and with my word the TV dies in a little explosion. From it, a grayish-white feather floats down to the carpet. Or a clump of my father's hair.

—Timothy Dodd

Counting by Mississippis

Only Clemons can tell you *exactly* what happened, but it all started with his family undergoing a kind of culling. It was the cruelest act of nature I'd ever seen up-close, and completely beyond my grasp at the time, being as I was, in those days, a selfish bastard, which is also part of this story. The core of the matter was this: one of Clemons' family members had died each year, for five years in a row—wife, sister, mother, father, and his own son— until he was down to only the ones he didn't like. Each death was by illness, disease, or some variety of cancer. Stroke took his son. Pneumonia fell Clemons' tall father.

Clemons clung to his sanity for far longer than most would have.

Drinking, of course, occurred—alcohol abuse of prodigious scale—and anyone who knows anything about that knows that it only serves to deepen depression and further disorient the mind, which is exactly what happened for Clemons. He confided in me one afternoon during a sojourn at our respective mailboxes. He told me he was feeling, to use his word, "unmoored" from reality. He also said something about having only "a tentative grasp" on things.

"You need to find something to do, my friend," I told him. "A hobby or something. You got anything you like to do—other than, you know, what you're doing presently?"

He smiled at me and nodded. If I'd known him better, if I had been a better neighbor, I might have intervened at this time. If I had been more like Old Linda, our across-the-street neighbor, I could have been more help to him. But we weren't much more, really, than mailbox compatriots, and I hadn't, at that point, cleared out the space in my stunted life for another human and his immense grief. We'd shared an odd beer together, in my or his yard, while bemoaning chinch bugs and dollar weeds—but that had been the extent of it. Old Linda, though, would eventually help me bring proper bearing to all this. That's part of the story, too.

"Last night," he said, while slapping a short stack of envelopes on his leg, "I got so drunk on Jameson that I blacked out and woke up this morning with a blurred, gauzy vision of myself peeing into a loafer." He lowered his head and brought it back up with a twisted smile. "I got out of bed and walked over to the closet." He pointed to his left, as if a closet might be standing there in the yard. "There on the floor of the closet were two brown loafers, one of which was several tones darker than the other. I didn't dare touch it. Just left it there." He squinted at the sun, "Once you've pissed in a shoe," he said more to himself than to me, "you're in uncharted territory."

"That's what I'm talking about," I said. "You need to find something—some activity or task—to do to take your mind off things." I don't know if it was good advice, but I was trying to be neighborly, and it seemed to me like a sensible suggestion.

Later that morning, still drunk, he got into his pickup and drove slowly around the neighborhood. Two days later, he related the following to me:

"I rolled to the intersection and turned left onto Raintree Circle. I passed that boy named Avery on his BMX and waved at him. Believe it or not, that boy showed me his middle finger and called me a *creepy fucker*. In retaliation, I told him he had a girl's name, which I oughtn't have done, and the kiddo threw a rock at my truck, but missed." This, Clemons told me, made him cry uncontrollably.

"I couldn't help it. The mourning tore loose of me," said Clemons. He wanted to pull over but he could not do so without pulling into someone's yard, so he kept driving. Finally he came upon a yard sale and, as he rolled by, he saw what looked like an old bike. He pulled to the side and got out and walked to the neighbor's driveway. It *was* a bike; according to Clemons, "a sweet old Cooper Velocrome" road bike. He haggled briefly with the turd selling it and bought it for fifty bucks. "I'll fix it up and sell it," he thought, "and it will keep me from going crazy." He was taking my advice, he told me. It would be a good distraction, something to stop him from venturing too deeply into *the farther territories* (what he'd come to call his nightly drunken journeys into the *internal oblivion*, wherein he brought out of himself and into the world-at-large staggering and sometimes terrifying incoherencies), some artifact of reality to keep him firmly rooted and present in the external world.

This is what *he* told me, in detail, the last time I spoke with him.

Clemons took the old bike into the garage and put it up on the mechanics bike stand, tightened it down, and took a step back. Even in this beat-up state, it was a beautiful thing to behold. His first real road bike had been a Cooper Velocrome. Cooper wasn't a great bike manufacturer these days—they'd sold out to Wal-Mart—but back in his day, the early 70s, when this bike was made, they had been a top bike manufacturer, and the Velocrome was a prime example of what an American company could do. It was a gorgeous bike. It had exquisite lines and a distinctly classic, almost Italian, look and feel to it. He knew he was going to enjoy fixing it up.

That night Clemons made empty a bottle of Jameson and woke up the next morning naked on the living room couch hugging a Virginia ham like a pillow. He puked three times while showering and had a dry waffle and a Heineken for breakfast. For half the day he did nothing but lie on his back in bed and stare at the wall. He took a brief nap, maybe thirty minutes, wherein he had horrific murder dreams. He got up and went into the garage and looked at the bike. "Fuck you in your rear derailleur," he said and walked back inside.

At dusk Clemons was finally hungry for an actual meal. He got out of bed and walked to the fridge whose contents consisted of one tallboy can of Heineken, a quarter pound of boloney, and a Virginia ham with crude, reckless bitemarks in it. He took out the beer and sat on the kitchen counter and drank it down. While he drank he thought: "I've got no use for boloney. The ham scares me. Drink this beer and go out into it. Fresh night air and some sensible victuals."

He went to the Italian place up the road from us, about a mile, and set at the bar and ordered a meatball sub and a Peroni. The sub was good. It was the perfect thing. The bartender came over and picked up the vacant plate.

"Seems like the days are coarse and revelatory, but unaccustomed," said Clemons to the bartender.

"What's that, sir?"

"Another Peroni would be amenable," said Clemons. He began to feel as if he could not control what he said. This had happened before. The "unmoored" feeling intensified. "Am I becoming a kind of werewolf?"

The bartender smiled and set the Peroni down in front of Clemons.

"This is the mangle of something reputable and once sincere," said the bartender.

Clemons shuddered, thought, "Oh shit!" and went for the beer, but it would not be taken up. He waved a hand into it and the contents churned like a little whirlpool. The bartender smiled at Clemons.

His teeth were perfect—but then his whole face changed. He became birdlike. Owllike, to be precise. The young man softly hooted at him.

"Goddamn," said Clemons. "You got some pretty feathers, boy."

"I was brought up on syncopation and everyday parables. It is the everydayness. It's just like Chekhov said." He winked a big, glassy owl-eye at Clemons. Then he started to cry.

"Heaven's sake," thought Clemons. "It's happening to other people too. We're all losing our minds. We're all mourners. We're all becoming something. I'm not alone." But he was alone, and he was projecting his insanity, as it were, on others.

It was harrowing and at times seemed impossible, but Clemons managed to pay the dinner bill. As he was getting up off his barstool the bartender asked him if he was okay, but, to Clemons, it came out as something sinister and threatening— a violent barn-owl screech.

That night he managed not to drink, but he didn't sleep either. He sat in a chair in his garage. Sometimes he stared at the bike on its stand and thought about what he'd do to fix it up. Other times he did nothing and thought nothing and was, as he told me, "the very void itself—a human blackhole."

To balance out his sleepless night of sobriety he drank the entirety of the following day. While the sun was out, he drank. He rationalized this drinking by sprinkling in household chores and yardwork. "At least I'm being productive," he told himself.

Clemons paused in his telling. Took a deep, desperate breath.

"You remember seeing me, around noon yesterdee?" I asked him.

He blinked at me.

"You were standing in the yard, in a pair of plaid boxers. Just standing in the middle of your front yard, kind of in a stance, like you were bracing yourself for a tackle."

I stopped to see if any of this registered.

"Seems like..." he said and then stopped.

"I asked you what you were doing and you said, 'Counting by Mississippis.'"

"Jesus," said Clemons in response. "Sorry you had to see that."

"You went inside after that, which I was glad for. Any longer and Old Linda might have noticed and called the police." Old Linda liked looking out her front window at the things that happened on our street. She was a widow. A window widow.

That night, Clemons told me, he had dreams of owls on bicycles. All kinds of owls. Barn owls, snowy owls, screech owls, horned owls, those little elf owls—all with long, muscular legs, doing circles and figure-eights on restored road bikes. Some owls spoke French and one, a particularly boyish owl, flicked him off—gave him the middle *feather*, as it were. Another owl, a brindle wearing a Saxobank jersey, peddled up to him, handed him a check for eight hundred dollars and said, "This here's for your trouble. The man what wrote it is dead. There's always someone dead, and the dead have to pay."

I told Clemons, my neighbor and mailbox acquaintance, that he might consider seeking some help. It was all I had left. What can you do for a man who's seeing obscenity-prone owls on bicycles? This was a mistake. I made a big mistake here. Truth is, I'm an asshole. A selfish asshole.

Today, as I write, it is Sunday. Here's what happened Saturday—yesterday—after Clemons told me about the owls. I hadn't seen Clemons since Wednesday, when he told me about the owl dream, and I was worried. Like I said: to my mind, we weren't the stop-by-for-a-visit type friends, so I was reluctant to knock on his door. Old Linda would wander over every once in a while, though. I'd see her knock, be let in, and not come out of Clemons' for nearly an hour. I often wondered what they did in there because I never heard Clemons do anything but joke about Old Linda, make bawdy comments about her, etc. I wondered, sometimes, did they do it? Were these occasional visits conjugal in nature? They were both about the same age and widowed. Old Linda, I said to myself. Sad, Old Linda. Why did we call her that, Clemons and I? She wasn't even that old. Maybe forty-eight. What had been her husband's name? I wondered aloud. Bob seemed right. Bob and Linda. Bob had died of—damn, I didn't even know. Stroke, heart attack....Clemons had gone to the guy's funeral, and I had not. Part of my aforementioned assholishness is that I can't imagine why someone would go to a funeral. You couldn't bully me into going to one. But Clemons had gone to Dead Bob's.

Had gone of his own volition. Clemons was not an asshole. I peeked out the living room window and glanced over at Old Linda's place. I had an idea.

Old Linda opens the door and smirks at me. Her whole attitude is lightly bemused, and almost knowing, like she'd been expecting me. I sigh and get into it. I point back towards Clemons' place.

"Linda," I say (almost say Old Linda), "I'm worried about Clemons. He's been struggling lately—you know why—and he ain't been out of the house in three days, since Wednesday." I pause, thinking she might want to interject. She does not.

"Anyway, you and Clemons seem pretty close, so I was hoping you might go over and check on him. He and I don't really visit with one another." Pause, again, and she's still smirking. "What do you think? You mind paying him a quick visit? He and I just weren't friends like that."

"You 'friends like that' with anyone?" she says.

This sort of blindsides me. I notice that Old Linda is still wearing a wedding ring. Bob gave her that. Dead Bob and Old Linda. Old Linder. Dead Borb. Jesus. What a fucking question...

"What're you getting at Linda?" I realize my tone is aggravated. "I just want someone to go check up on Clemons. Can you do that for me—for us—for Clemons?"

"Why can't you do it? It's a fairly simple task: walk over," she points across to his house, "knock on the door. If he answers, feel things out. Does he need help? Does he look okay? Does he need anything, does he want to talk? Sometimes people just need to talk, young man. If he does not answer the door, maybe you might want to call the police, the non-emergency number, of course—not emergency. Unless he's dead over there—*then* you can call emergency. Anyway, if you call the non-emergency, tell them of your concerns. Have you even tried calling his home phone? This is not complicated stuff here..."

Sounded complicated to me. Plus, she's talking to me like I'm a goddamn idiot, calling me *young man* and all. This is not going how I'd expected it to. "I don't have a number for Clemons," I say. It strikes me as odd that I don't have Clemons' phone number. OL condescends her whole body at me—it's like she's hovering over me now.

"Are you even *friends* with Clemons?" she says. "Come in for a second."

I decline her invitation in and stand on her stoop and wait for her to return.

She walks farther into her house, where her kitchen must be. She comes back holding a post-it note, hands it to me. It's Clemons' phone number, she tells me. "Give him a call," she says.

"You understand, don't you?" she says, as I'm walking away. "The poor man is being slowly murdered by death. A man—a person—can only take so much of it, of death."

Who knew Old Linda was all business like this? I think. She's got no softness to her. She's all jaggedness and sharp edges. She's a dark and stormy night, all to herself. And she ain't *old*, either. It occurs to me, in this stalled moment, that she's ageless. Timeless. There's something immortal to her. Something Pallas about her. Out of that moment, the truth shoots at me from somewhere, like a stray bullet, not meant for me. Friendly fire. It says: *you have not known death, jackass. Every person—every single person—important to you in life is still living and quite healthy and will not die for many years hence.* This realization, in contrast to Sad Clemons' and Immortal Linda's deep darkness, momentarily knocks the wind out of me.

At the end of Linda's driveway, I turn. There she still stands, at her home's threshold, hands folded in front of her, like a mother awaiting the return of a late child.

I hold the post-it up in the wind.

"Thank you," I say. "I will call and maybe go over."

She's statuesque, silent, and a kind of beautiful.

In my kitchen, I stand next to the phone, Clemons' number in hand, but I do not call. I feel, for some reason, acutely perceptive, and in thrall to it, the perception. I'm locked in. I can do nothing but perceive. I move over to the dining room chair and sit and let it wash over me like a swell on a grey day, and here is what comes, clear as a bell being rung, clear as a baby's cry in a quiet house, clear as a preacher's croon at the pulpit: *until you know death, you cannot fully know love.* And then there's a little addendum or postscript: *also, you are an asshole.*

This lyric whispered across the wind brings me to the brink of a tiny, private, welcomed madness. A madness of decency. I set the post-it on the table and pause, take a deep breath. I lock the front door and walk back out into the dusking day. I count as I walk across the green grass to Clemons' front door. So close, really. From door to door: ten Mississippis.

—Steve Lambert

About the Authors

Timothy Dodd is from Mink Shoals, WV, and is the author of the story collections *Fissures and Other Stories* (Bottom Dog Press) and *Men in Midnight Bloom* (Cowboy Jamboree) as well as the poetry collection *Modern Ancient* (The High Window). His stories have appeared in *Yemassee, Broad River Review,* and *Anthology of Appalachian Writers*; his poetry has appeared in *The Literary Review, Crab Creek Review,* and *Crannog,* among other places. Also a visual artist, Tim's paintings may be sampled on his Instagram page, @timothybdoddartwork. Find him also at timothybdodd.wordpress.com.

Steve Lambert was born in Louisiana but grew up in Florida. His writing has appeared in *Saw Palm, Chiron Review, The Pinch, Broad River Review, Cortland Review,* and many other places. In 2015 he won third-place in *Glimmer Train*'s Very Short Fiction contest and in 2018 he won *Emrys Journal*'s Nancy Dew Taylor Poetry Prize. He was also a Rash Award in Fiction finalist. He is the author of the poetry collections *Heat Seekers* (2017) and *The Shamble* (2021), the chapbook *In Eynsham* (2020), and the fiction collection *The Patron Saint of Birds* (2020). His novel *Philisteens* came out in 2021.

Sheldon Lee Compton is the author of nine books of fiction and poetry, including most recently the fiction collection *Sway* (Cowboy Jamboree Press, 2020) and the poetry collection *Runaways* (Alien Buddha Press, 2021). Cowboy Jamboree Press published his *Collected Stores* in 2021 and will publish his first nonfiction book, *The Orchard Is Full of Sound,* in 2022.